THIS LITTLE TIGER BOOK
BELONGS TO:

_____

_____

_____

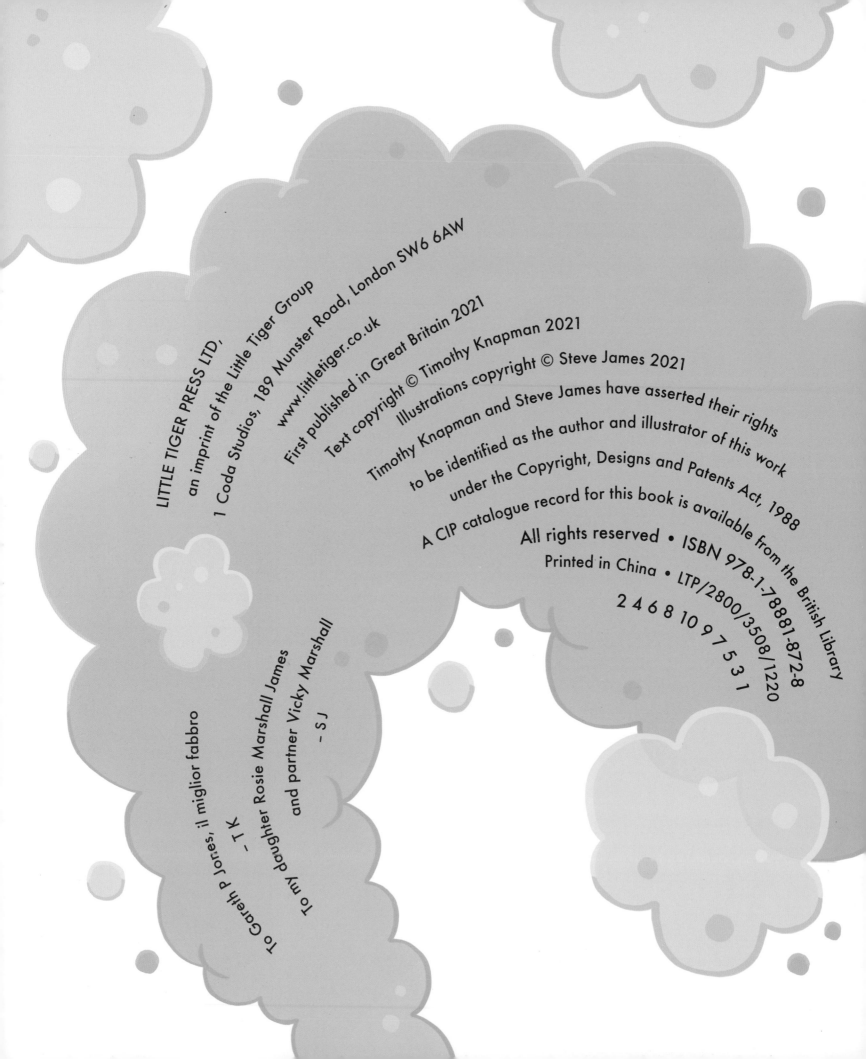

LITTLE TIGER PRESS LTD,
an imprint of the Little Tiger Group
1 Coda Studios, 189 Munster Road, London SW6 6AW
www.littletiger.co.uk

First published in Great Britain 2021

Text copyright © Timothy Knapman 2021
Illustrations copyright © Steve James 2021

Timothy Knapman and Steve James have asserted their rights
to be identified as the author and illustrator of this work
under the Copyright, Designs and Patents Act, 1988

A CIP catalogue record for this book is available from the British Library

To Gareth P Jones, il miglior fabbro
– T K

To my daughter Rosie Marshall James
and partner Vicky Marshall
– S J

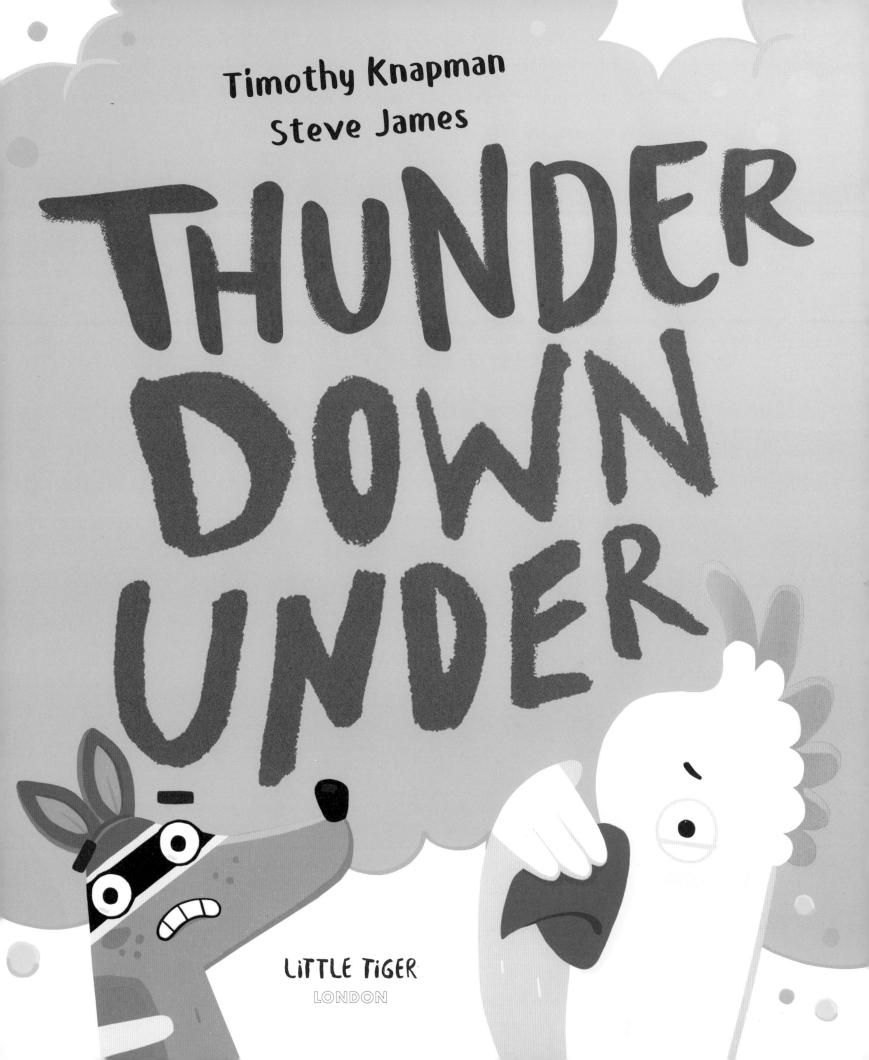

Timothy Knapman

Steve James

THUNDER DOWN UNDER

LITTLE TIGER
LONDON

On the first day of summer, the air smelled so sweet
That the animals rushed out to play in the heat.

Not seeing that **Numbat**

was looking for food,

They trampled straight past him,

which was rather **RUDE**.

They played very

ROUGHLY,

they STOMPED
on the ground,

When suddenly

there was a . . .

It was tree-flapping clattery, ear-wibbling loud!

And after it rolled in this STINKY GREAT CLOUD.

One whiff and at once all the animals started

To whisper and wonder — "MY GOODNESS! WHO'S FARTED?"

"ASK ME!" said the neat little **numbat**, "I know
Just exactly who gave
their bum **trumpet** a blow."

But nobody listened,
nobody at all –
For **who** pays attention
to someone so small?

So the wombat piped up
(he liked being in charge):

"This **whiff** must have come

from a rump that is

LARGE.

It's **big**
and it's **grand**

and that's how I can tell . . ."

"That the **emu's** the one who let out this

BAD SMELL!"

The **emu** was angry and wrinkled her beak.

How **dare** you suggest that was **my bottom squeak!**

"I am tall and I'm wise, so of course I know who
Has parped very rudely – it's you, Kangaroo!
All that **bouncing** and **bumping**, it loosens the bot."
But the kangaroo snorted,

**What cheek!
I did not!**

"ASK ME!" said the **numbat** –

he **jumped** up and down.

"I'll tell you **exactly** who turned the **AIR BROWN**."

But nobody **LISTENED**, nobody at all —

For who pays attention to someone so **small**?

So the **kangaroo** told them,
"Hey, I know the chap
Who's ruined our day with
this **huge backside flap!**

It's not hard to work out,
just **sniff** and – by jingo –
You'll know it's our friend here,
the dastardly **DINGO!**"

The dingo said,
"Strewth, mate!

You're really way off
If you're saying that I made
that ripe trouser cough!
Now I know

who farted

(prepare for a shock) . . ."

It's bubbly and SWAMPY: it must be the CROC!

But the croc said,

The **wallaby just** cut the **cheese**.

No I didn't! It's Possum! It's HER REAR-END SNEEZE!

I tell you the **bandicoot** rang his BUM BELL!
No way, it was Platypus's PONGY BOT SMELL!

"Oh **WHY** won't you listen?!" the **numbat** called out.

"And then you will **know** and I won't have to **shout!**"

But nobody listened, nobody at all –
For **who** pays attention to someone so **small?**

So they just kept on arguing: some thought a shark
Was the one who had let out the loud bottom bark.
They all knew a noise like that just had to come
From a very **important** – and large – **creature's**

BUM!

Then suddenly, **shockingly,**
SHAKINGLY LOUD

A fresh fart erupted
and silenced
the crowd.

They looked at each other
in horror and **wonder**
At this latest rumble of

thunder
down
under.

They **all** held their noses
and turned round to see . . .

. . . The numbat who, laughing, said,
"Yes! It was me!

I blew that

BUTT

SNEEzE!

And I warmed the seat!

Yes, I let it rip –
it was my

BOTTY

TwEET!

But you all ignored me because of my size,
I hope that you've learned something from this surprise.
We small ones are just as important as you
And anything you can do, we can do too!
We're brainy and brave, we have plenty of heart,
And – most importantly – boy, can we
fart!"

Then he **trotted** away with his **tail** in the air,
And **everyone** just had to **stand there** and
STARE.

So the moral is perfectly clear
– don't you think?
You're never too little to kick up
A STINK!

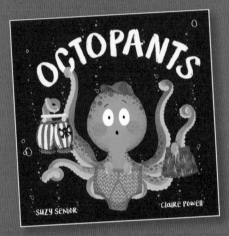

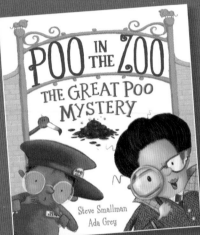

POO IN THE ZOO
THE GREAT POO MYSTERY

Steve Smallman
Ada Grey

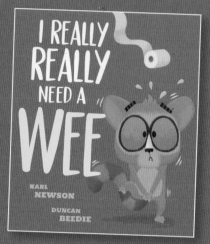

I REALLY REALLY NEED A WEE

KARL NEWSON

DUNCAN BEEDIE

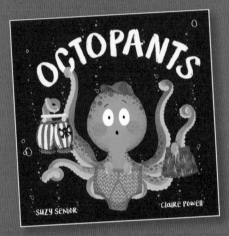

OCTOPANTS

SUZY SENIOR   CLAIRE POWELL

More thunderously funny books from Little Tiger . . .

THE Monkey with a Bright Blue Bottom

STEVE SMALLMAN   NICK SCHON

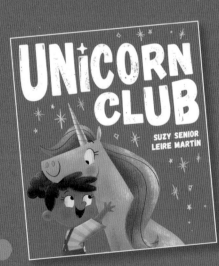

UNICORN CLUB

SUZY SENIOR
LEIRE MARTIN

NOW YOU SEE ME NOW YOU DON'T

Patricia Hegarty   Jonny Lambert

LITTLE TIGER

For information regarding any of the above titles or for our
catalogue, please contact us: Little Tiger Press Ltd, 1 Coda Studios,
189 Munster Road, London SW6 6AW • Tel: 020 7385 6333
E-mail: contact@littletiger.co.uk • www.littletiger.co.uk